Unicorn School

First-Class Friends

Willow started to back up when a
strong wind seemed to blow up
from nowhere. It swept into her,
knocking her off her feet.
"Willow!" she heard Sapphire gasp
from behind her.
The wind swept Willow straight
toward the edge of the cliff.
"Help!" she whinnied in alarm.

Linda Chapman lives in Leicestershire, England, with her family and two Bernese mountain dogs. She used to be a stage manager in the theater. When she is not writing, she spends her time looking after her two young daughters, horse riding, and teaching drama.

Books by Linda Chapman

MY SECRET UNICORN series

UNICORN SCHOOL series

FIRST-CLASS FRIENDS

THE SURPRISE PARTY

Unicorn School

First-Class Friends

Linda Chapman

Illustrated by Ann Kronheimer

SCHOLASTIC INC.

New York   Toronto   London   Auckland   Sydney
Mexico City   New Delhi   Hong Kong   Buenos Aires

ISBN-13: 978-0-545-05363-1
ISBN-10: 0-545-05363-3

20 19 18   18 19 20/0

Printed in the U.S.A.
First printing, September 2008

To Charlotte, Beatrix, and Damaris Ambery

Contents

Chapter One

Unicorn School

"Are we nearly there?" Willow, the small snow-white unicorn, whinnied eagerly as she and her parents cantered across a meadow of lush green grass in Arcadia.

Willow's mom, a beautiful light gray unicorn named Stardust, nodded. "It's just around the next corner."

Willow plunged forward in excitement.

"There's no rush, Willow!" her dad called. "The gates won't be open yet."

With an impatient snort, Willow slowed to a trot. She couldn't wait to get to Unicorn School! All the young unicorns in Arcadia went to boarding school when they were nine. At school they learned how to fly correctly and how to use their horns to do magic things like casting charms, healing wounds, and seeing into the future. *It's going to be great fun*, Willow thought.

She and her parents trotted up a hill. As they reached the top, Willow stopped dead and stared. The school

and its grounds were spread out in
the valley below.

"Oh, wow!" Willow exclaimed.

Unicorn School was an enormous
castle with big golden gates and
several pointed turrets. Its pearly
white walls glimmered, and purple
flowers with gold spots on their
petals dotted the grass around it.
Five tall elves with pointed ears
were standing in front of the golden
gates. They were wearing sparkling
silver uniforms. Unicorns swooped
down from the sky, their horns
glittering and their long manes and
tails swirling around them.

Willow watched in awe as the
flying unicorns landed effortlessly on

the grass. Some of them only looked about eleven or twelve, and yet they flew so confidently. She wished she could do it as well as them.

"Well, what do you think?" her dad asked.

"It's wonderful!" Willow exclaimed, looking at the castle and at the unicorns who were cantering up to one another and talking about their summer vacation. They all seemed so much bigger than her. Willow knew that she was small for her age— something her annoying older brothers usually teased her about.

"I wonder which of these unicorns are Year Ones like you," her mom said as they trotted down the hill toward the golden gates. "And which ones you'll make friends with."

Willow glanced around at all the other unicorns. She felt strangely shy. Usually she liked meeting other unicorns, but here they all seemed to know one another and have friends to talk to.

Her dark eyes fell on a big white

unicorn nearby. He was standing with a unicorn who looked as if he might be his father. They had the same silvery white horns, handsome straight noses, and thick dark gray manes.

I bet he's a Year Three at least, Willow thought, looking at the tall unicorn. She watched the way he was standing close to his dad's side and frowned. It was strange that he looked nervous, and he didn't seem to be talking to anyone the way the other older unicorns were.

The unicorn's father bent his head. "I'll leave you now, Storm," Willow heard him say. He glanced at the gates. The elves had started to bustle about, taking out registers. "It looks like the gates are about to open. Have a wonderful first semester here."

"Thanks, Dad!" Storm, the big unicorn, snorted.

Willow frowned. First semester! So he must be a Year One unicorn like her. But he looked so much older. Her mom nudged her. "We should go, Willow. The elves need to organize everyone into their houses."

"Houses?" Willow asked, wondering what her mom meant.

"All the unicorn pupils belong to a house—Star House, Moon House, Rainbow House, or Sun House," her mom explained. "You'll eat with the people in your house and share a stable with them, too."

"And later in the semester there will be competitions between the houses," her dad added.

"I wonder which house I'll be in," Willow said.

"Well, your brothers were in Rainbow House when they were at school, so maybe you will be, too," her mom answered. "Now good-bye, and be good."

"Of course I will be!" Willow replied.

Her dad chuckled. "That'll be a first!"

"Dad!" Willow stamped a hoof crossly.

Her father snorted softly. "You know I'm only joking. I'm sure you'll make us proud of you." He touched his horn to Willow's neck. She felt a tingle of magic flowing through her, and her nervousness faded.

She lifted her head, and her dark eyes glowed. "I *will* make you proud of me," she told them strongly. "I promise I will."

Her mom smiled. "Good-bye, Willow!"

Both Willow's parents touched horns with her, and then they took off into the air. Willow watched them swoop away until they became small dots in the blue sky. Now that her parents had gone, she suddenly felt very alone.

Three older unicorns walked past her. They looked about eleven. The one leading the group had dark gray legs and black eyes that sparkled mischievously. He nudged his friends. "Look at that teeny-tiny Year One."

One of his friends—a girl— smiled at Willow. "Isn't she cute?"

"I'm not cute!" Willow said, tossing her head. She didn't like

being called teeny-tiny or cute. She
was nine, after all!

The leader of the group walked
up to her. "Are you missing your
mommy and daddy?" he whinnied
teasingly.

"No," Willow replied. She was, but
there was no way she was going to
admit it to the older unicorn.

He looked at her for a moment.
He reminded her of her brother
Cassius. He had the same teasing
gleam in his eyes.

"Didn't you know," he said to her,
"Year Ones always go into school
first?" He glanced at the shut gates.
The elves were standing in front of
them, talking. "You just go up to

the gates and bang on them three times with your horn, and then the elves will let you in." He stared at her with wide, innocent eyes.

But Willow wasn't fooled. "Really? I think you left out the part about me having to turn a somersault first." She laughed and swished her tail. "As if I'm really going to do that. I'm not stupid!"

The unicorn's friends giggled, and he looked slightly taken aback. But then he gave an easy shrug. "Okay, maybe you're not!" he said, grinning back at her.

"Come on, Oriel," the girl unicorn said. "Let's go and find the others!"

The older unicorns cantered off.

They swerved around a crowd of
very grown-up-looking unicorns
who looked like Year Sixes.

"Slow down there!" one of the
elves called out. "No cantering in
front of the gates!"

Oriel and his friends ignored him.
Oriel put his head down and gave a
proud buck. The elf's face turned

red with rage. "Why, you—you . . ."

Just then, one of the other elves stepped forward and blew a long note on a bronze horn. He was wearing a green velvet hat with three corners, and looked like he was the elf in charge. As the horn's note floated out, the unicorns all stopped talking. When everyone was silent, the elf cleared his throat.

"All right, everyone, it is time to go into school. Can you all line up in your houses, please?" The other four elves stood in a line beside him. "Star House, Sun House, Moon House, and Rainbow House," the chief elf said, pointing to each of the elves in turn. "Year Ones, you will find out your houses when you go in, so I would like you to line up in front of me!" He took a list of names out of his pocket and unrolled it.

The unicorns moved into five separate lines. Willow trotted forward and found herself near the front of the group of first years. Oriel and his friends were jostling one another in the line for Rainbow House. The elf in charge looked like he was getting very angry with them. Willow turned around and saw Storm joining the line of Year Ones.

"Oh, for goodness' sake!" The elf in charge of Rainbow House bustled over. "What are you doing?"

he asked, angrily pointing at Storm. "You're not a Year One. You're far too big. Get out of that line right now!"

Willow saw Storm look embarrassed. "But—but I *am* in Year One," he said, his voice little more than a whisper.

The elf glared at him. "Don't be ridiculous! Of course you're not! Now, which house do you belong to?"

Storm looked very anxious. People were staring at him curiously. "I—I don't know. This is my first semester," he stammered.

"Right, that's it!" the elf exclaimed. "I've had enough of this!

Out of this line! You're going straight to the headmaster!"

Making Friends

O riel and his friends snickered.
Storm looked as if he wanted
to sink into the ground. Willow
couldn't stand it. "He *is* in Year One!"
she exclaimed, stepping out of line.
She was aware of everyone turning
to look, but she didn't care. "I heard
him saying good-bye to his dad," she

told the elf. "It *is* his first semester here!"

The elf frowned, and for a horrible moment Willow thought he was about to tell her off, too. Then, suddenly, another unicorn walked out of the line to stand at her side.

"It's true," a voice said timidly. "I heard him saying good-bye to his father, too." Willow glanced around. The unicorn who had spoken was very pretty, with a silver mane that swept almost to the ground and large dark eyes fringed by thick eyelashes.

Storm looked at them both gratefully.

Just then, the chief elf walked up to

him with a list. "What's your name?"

"Storm," the tall unicorn replied.

The chief elf checked his list and nodded. "I have a Storm listed here as being a new Year One. It appears you *are* in the correct line."

"I'm sorry," the elf in charge of Rainbow House said to Storm. "You

are so tall, I thought you must be a
Year Three playing tricks." Everyone
continued to stare at Storm until
the chief elf blew a long note
on the horn. Two of the elves
opened the golden gates.

"Year One unicorns, follow me!"
the chief elf announced.

He marched through the gates.

Storm fell into line beside
Willow and the other unicorn
who had spoken up for him.
"Thank you," he said to them as
the elf led them through the gates
and across a grassy courtyard.
"People always think I'm older
than I am. I'm Storm. What are
your names?"

"Willow," Willow replied.

"And I'm Sapphire," the pretty unicorn said shyly.

They all smiled at one another.

"It's weird actually being here, isn't it?" Storm said. "At school, I mean."

Willow knew what he meant. She'd thought about coming to

school so much, it was very strange to finally be there—and to know she wouldn't see her mom and dad again for ages.

"I wish my brothers and sisters were here," Sapphire whickered nervously. "I'm not used to doing stuff without them."

"How many brothers and sisters do you have?" Willow asked her.

"Six," Sapphire replied. "Two of them are older than me, and four of them are younger."

"Wow, I only have two brothers, and that's enough!" Willow said.

"And I don't have any brothers or sisters at all," Storm put in. "I can't imagine having six of them! It must be very noisy!"

"It is." Sapphire looked wistful. "I'm really going to miss them."

"Do you think we'll all be in the same house?" Willow asked eagerly. She might have only just met Storm and Sapphire, but already she felt that she would really like to be friends with them.

"Looks like we're about to find out!" Storm replied as they followed the elf through an archway in the courtyard into a large, walled field. At one end there was a table with a stone top. An old, very noble-looking unicorn was standing behind it. His body was snow-white, without even a speck of darker gray. Willow stared. Most unicorns had horns that were gold, bronze, or silver, but this unicorn's horn was striped in all three colors.

"That must be the Tricorn," Willow whispered. She looked at him in awe. Her brothers had told her that the Tricorn was the school's headmaster, and he knew more about magic than any unicorn in Arcadia.

"Quiet, please!" the chief elf commanded. He organized the Year Ones into a line in front of the Tricorn. The rest of the school trooped into the field and lined up behind them.

When all the unicorns were

quiet, the Tricorn stepped forward. "Welcome!" he said, his strong voice ringing out around the field.

Hardly a unicorn moved. The Tricorn's gaze swept over the Year Ones. "You will gain much from being at school, but you must be prepared to listen and learn." His eyes seemed to linger on each one. They all stood very still. "First, you must start by learning your houses." He stepped forward and touched his horn to the stone table. Willow saw it glow, and a list of names appeared on it in four columns of swirly writing.

"Please step out as I call your name," the Tricorn said. "In Rainbow

House: Starlight, Topaz, Willow . . ."

Willow's heart leaped, and she stepped forward. *Oh, please let Storm and Sapphire be in Rainbow House, too,* she thought.

"Sapphire . . ."

Willow exchanged delighted looks with Sapphire.

"Flint, Ash, Troy . . ."

Willow glanced around. Storm was looking worried.

"Storm," the Tricorn finished.

Willow felt a rush of relief as Storm joined her and Sapphire. She gave him a friendly nudge with her head, and Sapphire nuzzled him. He looked really pleased.

The unicorn named Troy, who was also in Rainbow House, edged closer to them. "Hi," he said. He was short and muscular and held his head proudly.

"Hi," they all whispered back, and smiled.

The Tricorn read out the names of the Year One unicorns in the other three houses. "And now it is time to go and find your stables," he announced. He lifted his head so his striped horn glinted. "School dismissed!"

Four older unicorns trotted up to the Year Ones.

"I'm Juniper," said one, a handsome dappled gray unicorn with strands of black running through his mane and tail. "We're Year Sixes, and we're going to show you the stable where you'll sleep and then give you a tour of the school. Will the Year Ones in Rainbow House please follow me?"

Willow and the other Year Ones in Rainbow House walked toward him.

Juniper smiled at them. "Come on! I'll take you all up to your stable!"

Chapter Three

Watch Out!

The eight Year Ones in Rainbow House followed Juniper out of the walled field and into one of the towers. A corridor wound its way upward. "The stable where you'll be sleeping is at the top of the tower," Juniper told them. "It takes a while to reach it walking up this way, but when you've learned to fly, it'll be much quicker."

"Will we all be together?" Sapphire asked Juniper.

He nodded. "There are eight stalls in each stable, one for each of you." He trotted along until they reached a round room with large windows and a door in the wall opposite.

"We're in the clouds!" Sapphire exclaimed, looking out the large windows.

Ash, one of the other unicorns, looked around in surprise. "Where's the stable for sleeping?"

"In the clouds," Juniper said with a smile. He touched his glittering

horn to the door in the wall, and it
swung open. On the other side was
a white, fluffy cloud. It had a short
tunnel running through the center
of it. At the far end was a large
room split into eight stalls, separated
by low walls. Windows had been
carved out of the cloud walls, and
each stall had a bucket of fresh
water and a large net of hay.

"That's your stable," Juniper told

them. "The second years are on the cloud above you; the third years above them. It's the same all the way up, with the sixth years being on the highest cloud at the top."

"Wow!" Willow said, and stepped into the cloud tunnel. The floor felt soft and bouncy under her hooves. She touched the walls of the tunnel with her nose as she walked through it. A wisp of cloud floated away like a piece of cotton wool. There was a silver nameplate hanging over the entrance to each stall. Troy was in the stall at the end on the right. Next to him was Storm, then Willow, and then Sapphire next to her. On the other side of Sapphire was Topaz, then Starlight, Flint, and Ash.

The Year Ones went into their stalls. The cloud on the floor was even softer and fluffier than the tunnel cloud. Willow giggled. "I can't wait to go to bed tonight!"

"This is cool!" Storm snorted.

"Do you want to look around the rest of the school now?" Juniper asked.

"Yes, please!" they all replied eagerly.

They followed Juniper back down the tower to the ground. "You've already seen the Assembly Fields," Juniper said, pointing with his horn toward the fields where the Tricorn had spoken to them. "And through here," he pointed at a nearby archway, "are the Moonlight Meadows."

He led the way through the archway. A large meadow was spread out in front of them. It had a glittering stream and shady trees around the edges. There were lots of unicorns in it, talking and grazing and flying. "This is where we eat and also where we come between lessons," Juniper said.

The school was huge. Juniper took them through the Charm Fields, where they would learn about charms, to the Sea of Silence, a still, silvery sea that edged onto a white sandy beach. Juniper pointed with his horn to the pinky-gray cliffs that rose up where the beach ended. "Those are the Rose Quartz Cliffs where you'll learn how to use your magic to see what's happening anywhere else in Arcadia." He cantered along the sand and up a steep path. There was a vast area of short grass and tangled bramble bushes at the cliff top.

"This is the Flying Heath," Juniper explained.

"What's that forest over there called?" Willow asked, pointing with her horn at a thick forest of tall trees that edged the Flying Heath.

"That's Bramble Forest," Juniper answered. "We go through it to get to High Winds Pass, where we sometimes play sports and have races. Come on. I'll show you."

The forest was thick and deep. The trees towered overhead.

"High Winds Pass is up here," Juniper said, turning off the main track and leading the way up a narrow, twisting path. "Year Ones are only allowed to go there with a Year Six or a teacher. It's very easy to get lost on the way."

They took several more bends, all the time going higher and higher. Willow could see what Juniper meant about it being easy to get lost! She was sure she'd *never* be able to remember the way up there on her own.

At last the path ended, and they

stepped out of the trees. The top of
the mountain was a large, flat area
of ground with a steep drop all
around it. The unicorns' manes
swirled around them as they stood
on the short grass.

"It's very windy!" Starlight said,
sheltering beside Juniper.

"It looks like a great place for
having races, though!" said Troy,
seeing the perfectly flat area of grass.

"It's fine in the summer when the
winds drop," Juniper replied.

Willow cantered to the edge of
the grassy area and looked down the
mountain. Storm trotted after her.
The sides were rocky and steep.

"Be careful!" Juniper whinnied.

"Sometimes there can be really strong gusts of wind up here. Don't stand too close to the edge, Willow."

Willow started to back up when a strong wind seemed to blow up from nowhere. It swept into her, knocking her off her feet.

"Willow!" she heard Sapphire gasp from behind her.

The wind swept Willow straight toward the edge of the cliff.

"Help!" she whinnied in alarm.

Storm to the
Rescue

Willow thought she was about
to be swept over the cliff,
but the next second there was a
flash of white and Storm plunged in
front of her, placing his body
between her and the cliff edge.
Willow knocked into him. She fell
to her knees.

"Are you okay?" he whinnied.

"Yes!" Willow said, and scrambled to her feet as Juniper came cantering over.

"Willow!" Juniper exclaimed anxiously. "I thought you were going to fall over the cliff!"

"So did I." Willow's legs were trembling with shock. If she'd been swept over the cliff edge, she would have been killed! She swung around to Storm. "Thank you," she said shakily.

"You could have been knocked over yourself, Storm," Troy whinnied. "You were very brave to do that!"

Storm looked pleased but a bit embarrassed.

"Come on," Juniper said worriedly. "If the winds have started coming in gusts like that, then it's too dangerous to stay here. We'd better go back. And just remember, no coming up here on your own," he warned them all.

"We won't," Willow said fervently. There was no way she ever wanted to go up to High Winds Pass again!

Juniper led them back down through the forest. When they reached the Moonlight Meadows, they heard the sound of a horn blowing. "It's almost lunchtime," Juniper told them.

An army of elves appeared carrying silver buckets of food. Each one had a unicorn's name on it. They put them onto five long tables that had round holes for the buckets. "This is our table," Juniper said, showing the Year Ones to the Rainbow House table. "The teachers eat there," he added, pointing to a table where some adult unicorns were already eating. He nodded to a tall, muscular unicorn with kind eyes. "That's the head of Rainbow House. His name is Atlas, and he teaches flying. You'll meet him later."

Willow found her bucket of food and plunged her nose in. Delicious! Bran, boiled barley, and oats, her favorite! Storm was next to her, and

Sapphire and Troy were opposite. Juniper joined the table next to Troy.

As they all began to eat, Willow saw Oriel, the teasing unicorn from Year Three, farther up the table. When his eyes fell on Storm and Willow, he grinned.

"Hey, it's Little and Large," he called out.

Willow smiled. She and Storm probably did look pretty funny together. After all, she only came up to his shoulder. She glanced at Storm, who looked uncomfortable. "Just ignore him. Oriel's only teasing," she said.

"Were you stretched when you were a foal?" Oriel called to Storm.

"Or did your parents plant your hooves in fertilizer to make you grow?"

The other Year Threes snickered. Storm hung his head.

"Oriel!" Juniper said sharply. "Stop teasing Storm, or I'll report you to Atlas!"

"All right. Don't get your horn in

a twist, Juniper," Oriel said, but he turned back to his food and stopped teasing Storm.

"So when do our lessons start?" Troy asked Juniper.

"This afternoon," Juniper replied. "I checked your schedule, and after lunch you have a magic charms lesson followed by a flying lesson."

Willow's ears pricked. Wow! Charms and flying! She couldn't wait!

After lunch, Juniper took the Year Ones in Rainbow House to join the other Year One unicorns in the Charm Fields.

"Enjoy your lesson," he told them.

"Thanks," they all chorused.

The charms teacher was a very slim unicorn with pale gray dapples and a tail that swept all the way to the floor. She smiled at them with friendly eyes. "Hello, everyone. My name is Damaris, and I will be teaching you about charms and curses. As I'm sure you all know, a charm is something that helps you or brings you good luck, and a curse is something that does something bad to you."

The unicorns all nodded.

"You can charm or curse an object so that when a unicorn wears the object or sleeps with it for a night, they will be affected by it," Damaris continued. "Curses are contagious, which means that you can catch them simply by touching another unicorn who has the curse."

Troy lifted his head to raise his horn. "Why do we have to learn about charms and curses? My father told me that unicorns shouldn't use magic like that; unicorns should use the magic inside them."

"Your father is completely right," Damaris replied. "But occasionally it is useful to know how to charm something, in case you need to help someone you can't be near enough to touch with your horn." She fixed the class with a stern look. "Unicorns, of course, should *never* use curses. We only teach you about them so you know how to avoid them. Now, today I'm going to teach you how to make a good-luck charm. Let's begin."

Damaris gave each of the unicorns an old metal horseshoe and explained how to cast a good-luck charm by touching it with their horns and imagining all sorts of lucky things. She told them that when the horseshoe was properly charmed, it would turn silver and glitter.

It was hard to do, but by the end of the lesson most of the unicorns had managed to make their horseshoes glitter a bit. Willow's horseshoe was one of the shiniest. "Well done," Damaris praised her as she collected the horseshoes. "It looks like you might be a natural at this."

Willow glowed with happiness. She liked being good at magic!

"Why can't we just do magic?" Storm asked. "Why do we need lessons? I've read that unicorns who live in the human world can do real magic as soon as they first turn into their magical unicorn shape. Why can't we be like that?"

"A very good question, Storm," Damaris answered. "The secret unicorns who live with humans are born with a lot of magic, so they don't have to practice in the same way we do." Damaris smiled. "However, one day I'm sure you'll all find it just as easy to do magic as the secret unicorns do."

Willow exchanged looks with Sapphire. She hoped so!

After the lesson, Damaris took them up the cliff path to the Flying Heath to meet Atlas for their first flying lesson.

The teacher began by organizing them into a line. "Flying isn't difficult so long as you are prepared to practice," he told them. "Soon you'll find it as easy as cantering. By the end of this semester you should be able to play games in the sky and have flying races. The important thing to remember is that you must believe you can do it, and when you get up in the air, just take things very slowly. No racing around until you can turn and land. Do you understand?"

They all nodded.

He made them practice taking off, flying a little way up in the air, and then coming back down. "The mistake unicorns always make is to fly too high before they're ready, and then they start crashing into things and losing control."

I can do this, Willow told herself. She took a deep breath. *Fly*, she thought. A shiver of magic ran across her white coat, her body seemed to get lighter, and then suddenly, she was rising into the sky rapidly.

Down, she thought quickly as she remembered what Atlas had said about not flying too high to start with.

She floated down to the ground. As she landed lightly she gave a pleased whinny. All around her, unicorns were rising up into the air and landing again. Troy was really good at it. He was going very high up, then coming down and landing perfectly. But no one seemed to be having problems, well, apart from Storm, Willow realized. He seemed to be finding it hard to get off the ground.

"You have to believe you can do it," Atlas told him. "Try harder, and give a little push with your back legs."

A look of determination crossed

Storm's face. He pushed down hard with his strong back legs and flew upward into the air. "Whoa!" he cried, his legs flailing. Several other unicorns had to land hastily to get out of his way.

"Come back down!" Atlas called to him.

But Storm didn't seem able to control himself. He shot backward.

Troy was just behind him. "Stop!" he shouted in alarm.

In an effort to avoid Troy, Storm tried to plunge forward and shot straight into Sapphire! She spun out of control. Her legs kicked, but she couldn't save herself. With an alarmed whinny, she crashed down to the ground.

No Good at
Flying

"Sapphire!" Willow whinnied.
Storm landed on his knees.
He scrambled up and cantered over
to Sapphire, who was lying on the
ground.

Atlas reached her at the same time.
"Are you all right?" he demanded.

The heavy landing had knocked

all the breath out of Sapphire. She
gasped for air. Atlas touched his
horn to her chest. His horn glowed,
and a second later, a look of relief
crossed Sapphire's face as Atlas's
magic began to work and her
breathing slowed.

Next, Atlas touched his horn to a
long scrape on her side. It healed
instantly.

"Oh, Sapphire, I'm sorry I bumped

into you!" Storm exclaimed unhappily. "I'm so big and clumsy."

"It's okay," Sapphire told him as she got to her feet and shook the dust from her coat. "It was an accident."

"I'm so stupid," Storm groaned.

"No, you're not," Atlas told him kindly. "You just need to learn how to use your strength properly. But you'll get better the more you practice."

"I'll help you, Storm," Troy offered. "We can practice in between lessons."

Atlas looked around at the others. "Come on, everyone, the excitement's over. Let's try again."

★

By the end of the lesson, everyone apart from Storm was able to fly a few yards into the air and then land without crashing. But Storm wouldn't go more than a few inches off the ground. He seemed very worried about hurting someone again.

When the lesson finished, it was time for a snack. As they all headed back to Moonlight Meadows, Oriel came cantering by. He grinned at Storm. "I just heard about your flying lesson. It sounds like you had a *smashing* time." He giggled at his own joke. "You have to be the clumsiest unicorn ever, Storm!"

Storm looked very awkward.

Willow glared at Oriel. "No, he's not!"

"Well, just so long as I'm not flying when he is!" Oriel replied. "I don't want to be bulldozed into the ground!" He laughed and cantered off.

Sapphire nuzzled Storm. "Ignore him."

Troy looked angry as his eyes

followed Oriel. "Don't worry. I'm sure you'll be great at flying soon."

But Storm didn't look convinced.

The next week raced by. There was so much for them all to learn— more flying and charms and curses, rose quartz gazing and healing, unicorn history lessons and lessons about the geography of Arcadia and the human world. Willow, Sapphire, Troy, and Storm became good friends. They had great fun together. But Storm was still having problems learning to fly. Whenever he flew more than a little way off the ground, he seemed to panic. To make it worse, the other Year One unicorns were all improving quickly. By the end of the week, Willow and Sapphire could turn and circle in the air, and Troy could dive and swoop like a Year Three. They could all fly up to their stable in the clouds, but they never did because they didn't want Storm to feel left out.

On Friday, when everyone was getting ready for a flying lesson, Storm hung back. "Are you coming?" Willow asked him.

"I have a sore back," Storm replied, avoiding her eyes. "Atlas said to rest in my stall."

"Can't you get Atlas or one of the other teachers to heal it?" Sapphire asked in surprise.

"Unicorn healing magic should only be used for serious injuries. I just need to rest," Storm whinnied. "See you later!" He hurried away.

"He doesn't look like he has a sore back," Troy said suspiciously.

"I think he's making it up to get out of the flying lesson," Willow declared.

"Poor Storm," Sapphire snorted. "He's really unhappy that he can't fly."

"He's not going to improve if he doesn't come to lessons." Willow frowned in the direction of the stable. "We should tell him he has to come and practice."

"Atlas will be really mad if we're late," said Troy, looking worried.

"I know," Willow whinnied. "But I think we should talk to Storm. Look, why don't you two go ahead and say I'm on my way?" The others nodded, and she set off for the stables.

When she reached the courtyard she stopped in surprise. Storm was standing on the far side, talking to another unicorn. It was Oriel!

Why was Storm talking to Oriel? Willow wondered. *Usually all Oriel ever did was tease Storm and make him feel uncomfortable.* Their backs were toward her. She edged closer and saw Oriel pass Storm something. She couldn't see what it was, but Storm took it in his mouth.

Oriel cantered off.

Storm turned and saw Willow. He looked very guilty.

"What did Oriel just give you?" Willow demanded, trotting over to him.

"Mind your own business!" Storm mumbled. And before Willow could say anything more he cantered away toward the stables.

The Silver Horseshoe

"Wait, Storm!" Willow whinnied. She cantered after him, but Storm was much faster. By the time she reached the top of the tower, Storm was already standing in his stall. There was nothing in his mouth, but Willow spotted a small heap of cloud at his feet.

Willow was panting for breath. "What are you hiding?"

"I don't know what you're talking about," Storm muttered.

Willow looked at the lump on the ground. "So what's that you're covering up?"

"Nothing," Storm said hastily. "No! Wait!" he exclaimed as Willow stepped forward and impatiently swept away the cloud with one of her front hooves.

A glittering silver horseshoe lay on the floor.

"Okay," Willow said slowly, looking up at Storm. "What's going on?"

Storm sighed. "It's a lucky charm," he admitted unhappily. "Oriel told me that if I sleep with it in my stall tonight, it will help me fly better tomorrow."

Willow was puzzled. "You know we're not supposed to use charms to help with our magic. And why would you trust anything Oriel gave you?"

"He came to say he was sorry for teasing me about my flying. He was really nice," Storm said. "He said he wanted to make up for the teasing by helping me."

Willow blinked. "Maybe he isn't so bad after all," she said. "But you still should not use the charm, Storm. It would be really wrong."

Storm looked longingly at the glittering horseshoe. "Perhaps if I just used it once, I'd learn what to do and then be able to fly without it." His voice dropped. "You don't know what it's like being so bad at flying, Willow," he snorted unhappily.

He looked so sad that Willow couldn't help feeling sorry for him. "Well," she said slowly, "maybe using it just once won't matter too much.

But after that you must *promise* to go back to flying using your own magic."

Storm nodded. "I will. I promise."

Willow realized how late she was for the flying lesson. "Look, I'd better go," she said.

"Please don't tell the others," Storm begged her. "They'll just laugh at me."

"They won't," Willow said. "But if you really don't want me to tell them, I won't."

"Thank you," Storm said.

And leaving him looking much happier, Willow cantered down the tower.

Luckily, Atlas was late for the flying lesson, too. With a rush of

relief, Willow joined Sapphire and
Troy.

"Is Storm okay?" Sapphire asked
anxiously.

Willow nodded. She longed to tell
Sapphire and Troy about the charm,
but she had to keep her promise to
Storm. "He's fine. He's going to
come flying tomorrow." She had an

uncomfortable feeling in her tummy. What was going to happen then?

At breakfast the next day, Storm was looking happy and excited. "You seem to be in a good mood," Sapphire said to him.

Storm nodded. "I can't wait to go flying today."

Sapphire and Troy looked astonished.

Willow gulped. She was beginning to have a seriously bad feeling about this. The more she thought about it, the stranger it seemed that Oriel would have given Storm a lucky charm. Farther down the table, she saw Oriel and his three friends,

Sorrel, Gemini, and Hera, watching them. Oriel whispered something, and his friends all giggled. Willow's feelings of unease grew.

After breakfast all the Year Ones made their way to the Flying Heath. "Today you're going to concentrate on changing speed when you're in the air," Atlas told them. "You need to learn how to go from slow to fast and then back to slow again."

Willow slipped into place beside Storm. "Good luck," she whispered.

"Thanks." He smiled at her anxious face. "Don't worry, Willow. I can tell this is going to work. I feel great today!"

Atlas told them to take off. Willow

felt her body sparkle with magic, and she pushed down with her back legs. She plunged into the sky. She loved flying! She wondered where Storm was and glanced around.

Storm was cantering up into the air. He looked confident and happy, but all of a sudden his body began to flip over.

"Whoa!" he cried as he turned upside down. The next minute he was spinning around and around in the sky.

He crashed into Flint, who whinnied in alarm and then gasped as he started spinning around, too. "Help! Atlas! I can't stop turning!" Flint whinnied. He spun into

Moondust, a Year One from Star House, and she started turning, too.

"What's going on?" she neighed.

Atlas galloped into the sky as Storm crashed into Topaz and Starlight, setting them spinning, as well. "Come down!" But as he spoke, Flint bumped into him, and the next second, Atlas was spinning around, too!

Within seconds, the sky was full of spinning, whinnying unicorns!

Willow hastily dived to the ground, avoiding the other unicorns. She suddenly realized what was happening. The horseshoe that Oriel had given Storm wasn't a good-luck charm. It was cursed!

"Help!" Sapphire gasped from above.

Willow was the only unicorn not spinning besides a group of older unicorns who were having their lesson at the far end of the heath. She galloped toward them. She had to get help!

As she got nearer she saw that the unicorns were third years. Oriel and his friends were hanging around near the outside of the group, watching the chaos among the Year Ones and laughing so hard they could hardly stand. Willow glared at them furiously. How could Oriel have done something like that to Storm? But right now she didn't have time to stop. She raced up to the teacher, a tall, skinny unicorn named Fabian. He was busy instructing a group of third years in diving techniques and hadn't noticed the commotion at the other end of the heath.

"Help!" Willow gasped, skidding to a stop beside him. "My class has caught a curse! Please help!"

Chapter Seven

Oriel's Dare

As soon as Fabian realized what was happening, he plunged into the sky, his golden horn glittering. He flew to the other end of the heath and touched each of the spinning unicorns with his horn, muttering a short spell as he did so. One by one, the unicorns stopped spinning. Looking very dazed, they all flew down to the ground.

"Thank you," Atlas whinnied gratefully to Fabian. He looked around sternly at the Year Ones. "Who was responsible for this curse? Someone could have crashed into the ground and been seriously hurt!"

No one said anything.

"Well?" Atlas demanded.

Storm stepped forward. "It—it was my fault," he admitted.

Atlas looked very surprised. "You? But why, Storm? Did you think it was going to be funny?"

"N–no," Storm stammered. "I didn't mean it to happen. Honestly. It was just . . . " He hesitated. "Well,

someone gave me a charmed
horseshoe. I thought it would help
me fly. But it must have been
cursed, not charmed." He hung his
head in shame.

"Storm! You should know better
than to try to improve your flying
through charms!" Atlas snapped
angrily. "Who gave you the
horseshoe?"

Storm didn't answer.

Willow glanced around at the Year Threes. She saw Oriel looking guilty. He slipped to the back of his class.

"Storm, if you don't tell me, you will go back to your cloud stable and stay there for the rest of the day. And there will be no sports all week!"

Storm looked upset, but he still didn't tell Atlas who had given him the charm.

"Very well," Atlas said coldly. "Go to your stable now. I'll be up to see you after the lesson has finished." Storm walked away unhappily.

Willow felt awful. It wasn't fair that he was getting into trouble because of Oriel!

"Okay, everyone, back to the lesson," Atlas said. "I think we'll do some talking on the ground while you all recover. And I hope the rest of you have learned a lesson—never use charms to help you in your flying!"

At break time, Sapphire and Troy joined Willow. "What are we going to do?" Sapphire said worriedly as they watched Atlas heading toward the cloud stables. "Storm will be in such trouble if he doesn't tell Atlas who gave him the horseshoe!"

"I don't understand." Troy frowned. "Who would have done something so mean?"

"I'll give you one guess." Willow glanced at Oriel, who was walking across the heath toward the school, snickering with his friends. Hot anger flashed through her. Oriel wasn't at all upset that he'd gotten Storm into trouble. Not caring that they were Year Threes and much bigger than she was, she trotted over to them and glared at Oriel.

"You think you're so funny, don't you?" she said.

Oriel grinned. "Yes, actually, I do."

Sapphire and Troy joined Willow as she stamped one of her front hooves furiously. "You've gotten Storm into real trouble," she told Oriel.

The older unicorn shrugged. "It's his fault for being so stupid. He shouldn't have taken the horseshoe."

"He's not stupid!" Willow exclaimed. "You're mean. You shouldn't have done it!"

"Ooh," Oriel teased. "Is he your boyfriend?" His friends giggled.

Willow was too angry to care. "Well, I think you should own up.

Storm is getting into even more trouble now because he won't say who gave him the horseshoe."

Oriel looked at her as if she were crazy. "I'm not owning up. *I'd* get into trouble then."

Willow felt like hitting him with her horn. "But it's *your* fault."

A sly gleam suddenly came into Oriel's eyes. "All right. I'll tell you what. I have an idea." He motioned with his head for Willow to walk away from the group with him.

She followed the older unicorn very warily. What was he up to?

"I'll confess," Oriel said, much to Willow's surprise. "But on one condition."

"What?" Willow said suspiciously.

"That you come with me to High Winds Pass and stand in the middle of it all on your own."

"High Winds Pass?" Willow faltered.

"Are you chicken?" Oriel smirked at her. "I heard you were so frightened when you went there on the first day that you couldn't even stand up."

"That's not true!" Willow said hotly. "I was knocked over by the wind!"

"Well, then, if you're not scared, you'll do it." Oriel challenged her. "I dare you!"

Willow didn't know what to say. She didn't want to go there, and she didn't trust Oriel. But if it would help Storm . . .

"All right," she said slowly. "But you *have* to own up afterward."

Oriel nodded. "Okay. Let's go after lunch. I'll meet you here. Don't tell anyone." And with a laughing whinny, he cantered back to his friends.

Troy and Sapphire questioned Willow all through lunchtime about what Oriel had said to her, but she refused to tell them. She didn't want them to come with her and maybe get into trouble, too. After lunch, she pretended she was going up to the cloud stables, but instead of heading to the courtyard, she cantered to the heath. She felt sick. She really didn't want to go up to High Winds Pass with Oriel.

Oriel was waiting. "Ready? Or have you changed your mind?"

Willow didn't want him to see that she was afraid. "Of course not," she replied scornfully, hoping her voice wasn't trembling too much. "Let's go!"

They cantered into the forest. Oriel led the way through the trees and up the twisting, turning path to the top of the mountain. As they got closer to the top, Willow could hear the wind whistling through the trees. A shiver ran through her as she remembered almost being blown over the edge of the cliff. She wished they could go back. *I'm doing this for Storm*, she reminded herself.

She raised her voice over the wind. "Where do I have to go?" she whinnied to Oriel.

"Just out onto the mountaintop," Oriel snorted. "Stand in the middle for a count of ten, and then the dare's done." He slowed down as they reached the top of the path.

"Go on. I'll wait for you here."

Willow cantered out onto the flat mountaintop. The wind was swirling around. She was almost blown off her feet. But she forced herself to the center of the pass and counted to ten. "Done!" she cried, looking around for Oriel.

But there was no sign of him.

"Oriel!" Willow whinnied.

There was no reply. Struggling against the wind, Willow made her way back to the path. Where had Oriel gone? There was no sign of him anywhere. "Oriel!" she whinnied again.

Oriel poked his head out from behind a tree near a bend farther down the path. "Tricked you! Now let's see if you can find your way back to school on your own." He turned and, with a flick of his tail, galloped away!

"No!" Willow neighed. There was no way she could find her way back without Oriel. "Come back!"

A faint laughing whinny floated up the path but Oriel didn't come back. Willow was on her own. The wind blew even more strongly.

Fear gripped Willow. She stepped toward the path. A gust of wind buffeted her, throwing her down to her knees. She staggered up and was almost knocked over again by an even stronger gust.

CREAK! A nearby oak tree bent in the wind. An earsplitting cracking noise came from its trunk.

Willow leaped back as the oak tree was ripped from the ground.

It crashed to one side with a splintering, cracking noise. Leaves and twigs flew into the air across the path. Willow's heart pounded. She could have been killed! Her mane whipped around her as she walked toward the oak tree. It had fallen across the narrow path and was blocking her way down the mountain. There was no way she could get past it! It was far too big for her to jump over, and she'd never be able to fly in this wind.

Willow tried to push her way through the trees on either side of the path, but there were so many brambles and thorny bushes that she got tangled up. She pulled backward, tugging her mane free. She couldn't get over the tree trunk, and she couldn't go around it. How would she ever get back to school?

The wind howled around her. Panic gripped her. She was trapped!

Chapter Eight

Trapped!

Willow's sharp eyes caught a flash of white on the other side of the tree.

"Oriel!" She gasped as he cantered up to the tree trunk.

Oriel looked shocked. "What happened?"

"The tree blew down," Willow

whinnied above the howling of the wind. "Why did you gallop off like that?"

Oriel looked very guilty as he peered at her though the tree's branches. "I just meant to scare you. I thought it would be a good trick to play. I was going to come back. I wasn't going to leave you here."

"But now I'm trapped!" Willow exclaimed. "How can I get out of here?"

"I don't know," replied Oriel. He tried pushing the tree with his shoulders, but it was much too big for him to move. "I'll have to get help!"

Willow felt panicky. What would

the teachers do when they found her there? All of the Year One unicorns knew they weren't allowed up to High Winds Pass on their own. Maybe she'd be expelled.

As if he could read her thoughts, Oriel spoke quickly. "I won't tell the teachers. I'll ask my friends to help. Will you be all right while I go back to school?"

Willow nodded bravely. "But be as fast as you can!"

"I will. See you soon!" And with that, Oriel galloped off.

It was horrible waiting for Oriel to come back. Willow paced up and down beside the tree trunk. Oh,

why had she come here? She just
wanted to be safe at school with her
friends. Tears pricked her eyes. What
if the teachers *did* find out, and she
was sent home? What would her
parents say? And what about
Sapphire and Troy and Storm? She'd
never see them again if she had to
leave.

Be brave, she told herself.

She took a deep breath and tried to gather her courage. She concentrated hard on Sapphire, Troy, and Storm. Oh, if only they were with her!

It seemed like ages, but eventually she heard the sound of whinnies on the path. She raced to the tree trunk. Above the roaring of the wind she could hear the sound of hooves. Suddenly, Oriel and three other unicorns came galloping up the path.

Willow stared. Oriel didn't have his friends with him. He had Sapphire, Troy, and Storm instead!

They raced up to the tree. "Willow!" they all whinnied.

"Oriel told us what happened," Troy said as he screeched to a stop. "He told us about bringing you up here as a joke."

"And about the tree blocking the path," Sapphire gasped.

"None of *my* friends would believe me," Oriel said unhappily. "They just thought I was trying to trick them."

"We hadn't seen you for ages," Storm said. "We were sure that what Oriel said must be true. Especially when he told us you'd come here to try to help me." He nuzzled Willow through the tree's branches. "We're going to rescue you!"

"Stand back!" Oriel told her, "and

we'll try to move the tree trunk."
He, Storm, Sapphire, and Troy began
to push the tree with their chests. It
moved a few inches and then
stopped.

"It's too heavy!" Oriel panted.

"Give me more room!" Storm
said.

They made a bigger space, and
Storm placed his strong shoulders

against the trunk. "All together!" he whinnied.

Willow watched anxiously.

"Push!" Storm exclaimed.

Storm's muscles strained, and he stepped forward step by slow step, pushing the tree out of the way until there was just enough space for Willow to squeeze through.

"Hurray!" she exclaimed as she came through the gap and plunged onto the path.

The other unicorns stopped pushing and whinnied in delight.

Willow nuzzled Storm. "Thank you, Storm!"

"I didn't do anything much," Storm said with a shy grin.

"We couldn't have done it without you," Oriel told him. "It's lucky you're so big and strong."

"You were great, Storm," Willow said.

"Yes," Sapphire said, stepping forward. "But we'd better get back before the teachers realize we're missing."

As they galloped into the trees, Oriel said, "It'll be quicker if we fly back."

"But—but I can't fly," Storm stammered.

Willow looked at his frightened face. "I bet you can. You were amazing just now when you moved the tree."

Storm hesitated.

"Have a try, Storm," Sapphire urged him.

"Yes, go on," said Troy.

"I bet you *can* do it," Oriel told him.

A spark of confidence flared in Storm's eyes as he looked around at them all. "All right," he said bravely. "I'll try!"

They lined up. "Okay. One, two, three!" Oriel said.

Storm pushed down with his back legs and took off beside Willow. "You're flying!" she whinnied as they rose into the sky.

"I am!" Storm gasped, wobbling beside her. He looked down, and for a dreadful moment Willow thought he was going to panic. She touched him with her horn. "You can do it," she whispered.

His eyes met hers. "Yes," he said determinedly. "I can!"

They flew side by side down the mountain. Swooping out of the woods, they flew across the heath. They landed and galloped into the Moonlight Meadows.

Oriel's friends were grazing together. They looked up in astonishment as Oriel cantered into the meadow with Willow, Sapphire, Troy, and Storm.

"So it was true," Gemini said. "You did need help."

"We thought you were joking!" Hera exclaimed.

"Well, I wasn't," Oriel told them. "Willow really was trapped behind a fallen tree. But Storm managed to move it. He was great! He's so strong!"

"It wasn't just me," Storm said modestly.

"No, but we couldn't have done it without you," Oriel told him.

"We'd have had to get a teacher if you hadn't been there, and then I'd have gotten into so much trouble," said Willow. She gave Oriel an angry look.

"I'm sorry, Willow," he said. "I should never have dared you to go to High Winds Pass. I wish I could make it up to you."

"Well . . ." Willow glanced toward Storm. "You could do what you promised. That would be a start."

Oriel nodded. "All right." He looked Storm squarely in the face. "I'm sorry about giving you the cursed horseshoe, Storm," he said. "It was a stupid trick. I'm going to tell Atlas it was all my fault."

"But you'll get into trouble," Storm whinnied in alarm.

"I know, but it's not fair if you get into trouble instead of me," Oriel told him. "Thanks for not telling Atlas I gave you the horseshoe. That was really good of you." He touched Storm's neck with his nose. "I'm sorry I've been teasing you. It's great that you're so big. I bet you'll win all the flying races for Rainbow House at the next sports day." He looked across the meadows to where Atlas was. "See you later." He grinned. "*If* I survive the telling off that Atlas is probably going to give me!"

He cantered toward Atlas. Willow

smiled. Maybe Oriel wasn't so bad after all.

"Let's go tell the others in Rainbow House what's been happening," Gemini said. "They should know how great Storm's been." Hera and Sorrel nodded, and the three of them trotted off.

"You'll be a hero when everyone hears about this," Troy told Storm.

"And just think, you can fly now!" Willow exclaimed.

Storm's eyes lit up. "You're right, I can! I flew all the way down from the mountain."

Willow grinned. It was great to see Storm looking so happy at last.

"Now we can race in the sky," Troy told him.

"And fly up to our stables," said Sapphire.

"I love being at Unicorn School!" Storm declared.

Willow looked around at her friends. She loved being at Unicorn School, too. So much had happened in the few days since they'd arrived. She wondered how many more adventures they were going to have.

Lots, the little unicorn told herself with a smile.

Here's a sneak peek at:

The Surprise Party

Willow's Great Idea

Willow trotted across the grass toward the Charm Fields. She didn't want to be late for her lesson. The sky was blue, and the sunshine glittered on her golden horn. A little way ahead of her she spotted one of her best friends, Sapphire.

"Sapphire! Wait!" Willow called.

Sapphire turned. She was a very pretty unicorn with a mane and tail that swept almost to the ground, a slender silver horn, and big eyes fringed by long dark eyelashes.

Willow cantered up to her. "Hi!"

"Hello," Sapphire muttered.

Willow frowned. Her friend looked sad. "Are you okay?"

"Yes." But there was a definite sigh

in Sapphire's voice, and her ears weren't pricked forward as they usually were. "I'm just feeling a bit homesick, that's all," she admitted.

Willow missed her mom and dad and two older brothers, too, but she loved being at Unicorn School so much that she never felt homesick for long. However, Willow knew Sapphire was different and that there were days when she really missed being at home with her six brothers and sisters.

"It's probably because I've been thinking about my birthday next Sunday," Sapphire continued. "It's going to be really strange not being at home for it. Whenever one of us has a birthday all the others put on a show for them. Everyone does magic tricks, and then we have a big birthday cake. It's lots of fun." She shook her head. "Oh, I'm just being silly, Willow. My birthday will be fine. Come on! If we don't get going, we'll be late for our charms lesson." She broke into a canter as if she didn't want to talk about it anymore.

Willow plunged forward beside her, but she couldn't stop thinking about what Sapphire had just said. She felt awful that Sapphire might be sad on her birthday. *I wish I could do something*, she thought. *But what?*